For Joey
– A. R.

To every child in this world who, because of war,
is deprived of a peaceful and playful childhood
– D. K.

Copyright © 2005 by Good Books, Intercourse, PA 17534
International Standard Book Number: 1-56148-473-3

Library of Congress Catalog Card Number: 2004019533

Text and illustrations copyright © Magi Publications 2005

Original edition published in English by Little Tiger Press,
an imprint of Magi Publications, London, England, 2005.

Printed in Singapore by Tien Wah Press Pte.

Library of Congress Cataloging-in-Publication Data

Ritchie, Alison.
What Bear Likes Best! / Alison Ritchie; illustrated by Dubravka Kolanovic.
p. cm.
ISBN 1-56148-473-3 (hard)
[1. Bear enjoys a day with nothing particular to do, but his friends seem too busy to play
with him. 2. Play--Fiction. 3. Bears--Fiction. 4. Animals--Fiction. 5. Friendship--Fiction.]
I. Kolanovic, Dubravka, 1973– ill. II. Title.

PZ7.R51155Wh 2005
[E]--dc22
2004019533

What Bear Likes Best!

Alison Ritchie

Dubravka Kolanovic

Good Books

Intercourse, PA 17534

800/762-7171

www.goodbks.com

Bear was sunning himself
on his favorite hilltop.
He loved days like this —
nothing in particular to do
and nowhere in particular
to go.

Buzzzzzzzzzz!

Buzzzz! A bee
landed on his nose.

"Get up, Bear," he said crossly.
"How can I collect pollen with bears squashing my flowers?"
"Sorry, Bee," said Bear, laughing.

Bear curled himself up

and roly-polied down the hill.

Roly-polying was one of his

favorite things to do.

Yippeeeeeeeee!

Bump! Bear landed on top
of something warm and furry.
"Oi!" gasped Mole. "How can I
dig holes with bears landing on me?"

Ooooof!

"I'll help you!" said Bear. And he dug
and dug and dug.

"Stop! Stop! STOP!" cried Mole,
as mud flew everywhere.

"Sorry, Mole," said Bear and he
hurried away.

Bear ran towards the river
and splashed into the water.
Splashing was one of his
favorite things to do.

Splish
Splash

"Hey!" grumbled Heron. "How can I catch
fish with bears chasing them away?"
"Sorry, Heron," said Bear and he
bounced off to play somewhere else.

Blah!

Bear hopped across the stepping stones, leaped on to the riverbank and ran into the woods. It was time for a back scratch. Scratching his back was one of his favorite things to do.

"Who's that?" said Fox, sleepily.
"How can I rest with bears
shaking the trees?"

"Sorry, Fox," said Bear.
"Do you want to scratch
too? It's so nice!"
But Fox did not
want to scratch,
so Bear clambered
up the tree.

Wheeee!

Wheeee!

Bear swung from branch to branch.
Swinging was one of his favorite
things to do.

Ooops!

Crash! Bear flew into a tree-trunk.
"Yikes!" cried Woodpecker, flying
high into the air. "How can I peck holes
with bears crashing into my tree!"
"Oops! Sorry!" cried Bear, jumping
to the ground.

"Bother! Everyone's too busy to play," Bear thought. "Oh, well!" He skipped through the woods, along the riverbank, across the field and back to his favorite hilltop.

Bear lay sunning himself on the hilltop.

Suddenly he heard a loud BUZZZZZZZ!
"Oh no! I'm in trouble again," he thought.

He saw all his friends coming towards him.

"Bear," said Bee, "you're very big..."

"And heavy," said Mole.

"And noisy," said Heron.

"And pesky," said Fox.

"And clumsy," said Woodpecker...

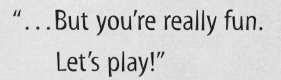

"...But you're really fun.
Let's play!"

"Hoorah!" cried Bear.
Because playing with his friends
really was his favorite thing to do.